Stand Up, Speak Out
No Regrets

By

Tequila Smith

Dedication

To every teen who's ever felt unheard, unseen, or underestimated—

This is for you.

Your voice matters. Your courage inspires.

Never be afraid to stand up, speak out, and live without regrets.

Acknowledgment

First and foremost, I thank God for the purpose placed on my heart, and the passion to walk it out through the power of words.

To my family and friends — your support fuels my journey. To the educators, mentors, and advocates, who stand beside young people daily, thank you for creating safe spaces for voices to rise.

A special thanks to the teens who inspire this work — you are bold, brilliant, and unstoppable. Keep using your voice to change the world.

About the Author

Tequila Smith is a passionate children and teen's author, devoted to empowering the next generation through bold storytelling, vibrant representation, and messages that matter. She is the creative force behind the Igniting Bright Futures Collection, which includes *Dream Big Young King*, *Today A Princess, Tomorrow A Role Model*, and *Wrapped In Gold*. Also, her latest children's book, *The Dragon I'm Slaying*.

With *Stand Up Speak Out No Regrets*, Tequila expands her mission by speaking directly to teens — encouraging them to use their voices, take up space, and walk confidently in their truth. Through each page, she seeks to remind young people that their stories are powerful, and their words can ignite change.

Other books by Tequila Smith that are already published and ready for the readers to grab as well as any future projects:

Dream Big, Young King

Wrapped in Gold

Today, A Princess. Tomorrow, A Role Model

The Dragon I'm Slaying

Stand Up Speak Out No Regrets

Melody and Song *(up-coming project)*

Table of Contents

The Ride or Die Dilemma

Jamal had always believed in loyalty. Growing up, he and Marcus had been through everything together. So when Marcus pulled out his older brother's car keys with a smirk, Jamal's heart skipped a beat.

"Come on, man. Just a quick spin," Marcus said, twirling the keys.

Jamal hesitated. "Bro, your brother's gonna kill you."

"Nah, he won't even know. Y'all coming or not?" Marcus challenged.

The other guys hyped Marcus up, pushing Jamal toward the car. He could feel the weight of their expectations. Not wanting to seem scared, he slid into the back seat.

As the engine roared to life, the thrill of rebellion filled the air. They sped down the street, laughing and blasting music—until flashing blue lights filled the rearview mirror.

"Crap," Marcus muttered, his hands tightening on the wheel.

Panic shot through Jamal's veins. "Pull over, man. Just pull over!"

Marcus tried to swerve onto a side street, but it was too late. Sirens wailed as an officer's voice echoed through a speaker: "Turn off the vehicle. Hands where we can see them."

Jamal's stomach churned as he realized what was happening. They were about to be in serious trouble.

His mind screamed, "I could've stopped this. I should've spoken up."

The car slowly came to a stop, and Marcus slammed his hands on the steering wheel, cursing under his breath. The officer's voice crackled again. "Step out of the vehicle. Slowly."

As they both stepped out, Jamal couldn't help but feel the weight of the situation. This wasn't just about getting caught. This was serious. They could be arrested, or worse—Marcus's brother could press charges. The officer asked for ID, and as Jamal handed his over, he saw Marcus's eyes dart nervously, calculating his next move.

Once the officer returned and let them off with a warning, Marcus let out a shaky breath, trying to play it cool, but Jamal was fuming inside.

"I can't believe you did that," Jamal said, his voice tight with anger.

"What are you talking about?" Marcus replied, his usual swagger fading. "We're fine, man. It's just a warning."

"No, it's not just a warning, Marcus," Jamal snapped. "You took the car! You were the one who decided to just drive off like everything was a game! Now we're lucky we didn't end up with charges or worse."

Marcus looked away, a hint of defensiveness creeping into his expression. "I didn't hear you stopping me. You didn't say anything when I pulled the keys out."

Jamal's heart started to race, and his voice cracked with frustration. "You're seriously gonna put this on me? You're the one who snuck the keys, who drove off like it was no big deal. I told you your brother would kill you if he found out! But you still went and did it."

Marcus stepped closer, his face flushed. "So what, you think I'm just supposed to be the only one who gets blamed? You could've said no. You could've told me to stop. But you didn't! You sat there in the back like everything was fine, just waiting for me to screw up so you could blame me when it all went wrong."

Jamal felt a sharp sting in his chest. "I didn't know you were gonna get us in that deep. I thought it was just gonna be a quick ride! But now look at us—staring down a cop because you thought it was a game. I trusted you to be smarter than that."

Marcus's jaw clenched, and for a moment, the silence between them was deafening. Finally, he let out a long sigh. "Man, I'm sorry. I just... I wasn't thinking. I wanted to show off, you know? I didn't mean for it to go like this."

Jamal exhaled, his anger simmering down. He knew Marcus didn't always make the best choices, but that didn't mean he had to cover for him every time. "You're lucky it wasn't worse. But next time, I'm speaking up. If you do something stupid like that again, I'm not riding with you."

Marcus looked at him, a mixture of guilt and gratitude in his eyes. "I get it. I'm sorry, bro. For real."

As Jamal walked away, he thought about the whole situation. Marcus had messed up, but Jamal knew he hadn't exactly been blameless either. He hadn't spoken up when he should've, and that's what made the whole situation worse.

It was a lesson learned the hard way. Sometimes, loyalty meant holding your friends accountable—not just backing them up when things went wrong. And next time, Jamal would speak up.

Moral:

True friendship means holding each other accountable, even when it's uncomfortable. Don't let loyalty blind you to the consequences of bad decisions. Speak up before things go too far, because real friends help each other avoid making mistakes that could change everything.

The Party Pressure

Mia scanned the party. The music thumped through the house, and the air smelled like sweat and alcohol. She wasn't even supposed to be here, but Jenna had begged her to come.

Jenna, already tipsy, shoved a red cup into her hand. "Just one drink, Mia! You never loosen up."

Mia glanced around. Everyone else was drinking and laughing. Would one sip really be so bad?

Then she thought about her mom's voice warning her about situations like this. She thought about her future, her college dreams, and the car keys in her pocket.

"Nah, I'm good," she said, putting the cup down.

Jenna rolled her eyes and wandered off with another group. Mia felt a pang of guilt—was she being lame?

Shaking off the feeling, she left early.

The next morning, her phone buzzed.

Jenna's in the hospital. Alcohol poisoning.

Mia's stomach clenched. If she had been more forceful and convinced Jenna to stop, would she be okay?

She had made the right choice for herself, but she couldn't shake the feeling that she should've done more.

Moral:

Saying no isn't always easy, but it can save lives.

Screenshot Regret

Jaden was lying on his bed, scrolling through his class group chat, when a new message popped up.

It was a picture—of a girl from their school. A private picture.

"Whoa," one of the guys typed.

"Yo, send that to me," another replied.

Jaden's stomach churned. This wasn't a joke. This was someone's life.

"This isn't right," he finally typed. "Y'all wouldn't want this happening to your sister."

Some of his friends groaned. "Man, relax. It's just a picture."

"No, it's someone's life," Jaden shot back.

The messages stopped. The next day, he discovered the girl's parents had reported the photo. The school was investigating.

A few of his friends were getting in serious trouble. Expulsions. Police involved.

Jaden exhaled, relieved he had done the right thing before things spiraled even further.

The girl whose photo had been shared was Emily, a quiet, introverted student who kept to herself. When she found out what had happened, she felt her world shatter. It wasn't just the violation of her privacy—it was the betrayal. She had trusted someone, and now her moment was being spread around like it was nothing more than entertainment.

At first, she was numb, her mind racing with disbelief. "How could this happen?" she thought. "Why me?" But soon, that numbness turned into a deep, crushing sense of shame. It was like every step she took at school felt like it was under a spotlight, everyone's eyes on her, judging her. She wished she could disappear, melt into the walls, but she couldn't. The world had seen her in a way she wasn't ready to share.

Her phone buzzed. Another message. It was from one of her friends: "Are you okay? I heard what happened." Emily didn't know how to respond. She felt so exposed, like every part of her had been laid bare without her consent. She didn't want to answer, not because she didn't appreciate her friend's concern, but because she didn't even know what she felt anymore. She didn't know how to make it stop, or if it even could.

The days that followed were a blur of whispered conversations in the hallways, eyes darting away when she walked by, and the unbearable weight of the situation. She couldn't escape it.

But then, Emily remembered something her mom had told her when she was younger: "You're stronger than you know." Emily clung to that thought as she worked up the courage to talk to someone about it. She went to her counselor's office, her hands shaking as she knocked on the door.

Her counselor, Mrs. Jacobs, welcomed her in, sensing the pain in her voice before Emily had even said a word.

"I don't know what to do," Emily admitted, her voice barely above a whisper. "Everyone knows. I feel... dirty. Like I'll never be okay again."

Mrs. Jacobs listened carefully, reassuring her that what had happened wasn't her fault. She explained the steps the school was taking to address the issue, and most importantly, she reminded Emily that there were people who cared about her, and she didn't have to go through it alone.

With Mrs. Jacobs' support, Emily began to see the situation in a different light. It wasn't her fault. It wasn't her responsibility to carry the shame. She was the victim here. It took time, and it was far from easy, but slowly, Emily started to rebuild her confidence.

As for Jaden, he had no idea how much his decision had helped. He hadn't known Emily personally, but his choice to speak up had indirectly saved her from even more pain. When the school investigation started, Emily's parents expressed their gratitude to Jaden's family. The boys who had shared the photo faced serious consequences, as they should.

Emily learned a tough lesson, one that no one should have to learn, but it also taught her the power of speaking out. She couldn't change what had happened, but she could make sure it didn't define her. And when it was all over, she held her head a little higher, knowing she had found her strength.

Moral:

Sometimes doing the right thing means standing up, even when no one else is. It's easy to follow the crowd, but in moments of pressure, the courage to speak up can change someone's life for the better. And if you're ever the one hurt, remember: it's never your fault, and there is always help to be found.

The Silent Bystander

Luis kept his head down as he walked the crowded hallway. He hated drama.

Then he saw it—Darren, an older student, cornering Tyler near the lockers.

"Just look at your shoes, man. What are those? Yo, you're a nerd for real," Darren sneered.

Tyler's eyes darted around, desperate for help. But everyone kept walking, pretending not to see.

Luis felt his heart pound. If he stepped in, Darren might turn on him.

But if he didn't, Tyler was on his own.

"Yo, Darren, leave him alone," Luis blurted.

The hallway went silent. Darren turned, sizing him up.

"Or what?"

Luis' voice wavered. "Or I'll tell the principal."

A teacher suddenly appeared, catching the last part of their conversation. Darren backed off, grumbling under his breath.

Tyler mouthed, "Thank you."

Luis exhaled. He had done the right thing. Even if it was scary.

Moral:

Silence allows bullying to continue. One voice can make a difference. The time is always right to do what's right. Nobody can do everything, but everyone can do something.

The Cheat Code

Rachel's heart pounded as she stared at the history test. She had studied—but these questions were way harder than expected.

Olivia nudged her paper closer. "Just copy a few. No one will know."

Rachel's stomach twisted. She was already struggling in this class. If she failed, her GPA would tank.

But then she thought about the consequences. Getting caught. Losing her scholarship chances. Disappointing her parents.

"I can't," she whispered.

Olivia frowned but turned back to her test.

Later, Rachel saw Olivia in the hallway, her face red.

"I got caught," Olivia muttered. "Zero for the whole test."

Rachel's stomach dropped. She felt a pang of guilt for not helping, but at the same time, relief flooded through her. She hadn't cheated. A failing grade could be fixed with extra credit or a retake. But a ruined reputation? Not so easily.

When Rachel received her test back the next day, her heart sank. A 72%. It wasn't great, but it wasn't the worst. She'd worked hard on it, and while it wasn't the grade she wanted, at least she knew it was honest.

But then the consequences started to hit. Olivia's situation spread like wildfire through the school. "Did you hear Olivia cheated on the history test?" whispered one of Rachel's friends. Another girl added, "I heard she's in big trouble. A zero for the test, and she might get suspended."

Rachel couldn't help but feel bad for Olivia, but at the same time, she couldn't shake the feeling of gratitude for sticking to her morals. She had avoided the immediate consequences, but soon she started to see the bigger picture. Olivia had earned her punishment for a reason—cheating wasn't a shortcut, and it wasn't worth it.

As for Rachel, her teacher called her after school a few days later to talk about her grade. Mrs. Turner, her history teacher, had noticed the improvement in Rachel's effort, and she encouraged her to keep pushing.

"I know you're capable of more," Mrs. Turner said with a warm smile. "Keep working hard, and your grades will reflect that."

Rachel couldn't believe it. She'd taken the hard road, but the encouragement made it feel worth it.

The real test came a few weeks later. The midterm exams were approaching, and Rachel knew she had to double down. She studied harder than she ever had before, using the skills she had learned in other subjects, and working with her classmates when needed. She didn't want to be in a position where she had to choose between integrity and success again.

When she got her midterm results back, Rachel felt a weight lift off her shoulders. A 92%. It wasn't perfect, but it was a massive improvement. And more importantly, it was all her work.

The moral support from her teacher helped Rachel realize that doing the right thing, though tough at times, was the best path forward. As for Olivia, she'd faced the full consequences of her actions—her scholarship had been at risk, and she was placed on probation. But as Rachel found out later, Olivia had learned from her mistake, too.

Rachel never forgot the lesson she had learned that day: shortcuts might seem tempting, but integrity matters. And the right choices lead to long-term success.

Moral:

Integrity matters. A shortcut today can lead to failure tomorrow. Sometimes doing the right thing means facing challenges, but it will always lead to personal growth and success in the end.

The Fake ID Fix

Carlos had always thought of himself as a good kid. He didn't drink, didn't get into trouble—he just hung out with his friends and went along with their jokes. So when Ryan pulled out the fake ID and suggested they buy alcohol "just to see if it works," Carlos didn't think much of it.

"Dude, what's the worst that could happen?" Ryan laughed, waving the card.

Carlos had a bad feeling, but he stayed quiet. He watched as Ryan and Marco strutted into the store, snickering. A minute passed. Then two. Then—sirens.

Carlos' stomach dropped as red and blue lights flashed outside the store. The clerk must have called the police. His friends were marched out, hands behind their backs.

Carlos wasn't inside. He didn't hand over the ID. But as he stood frozen on the sidewalk, heart hammering, he realized something: he could have stopped this. One word, one warning, and none of this would be happening.

The next day, Ryan and Marco were suspended. Their parents were furious. Their futures—suddenly uncertain. Carlos lay awake that night, staring at the ceiling, vowing he'd never stay silent again.

Moral:

Just because you didn't participate doesn't mean you're innocent. Speak up before it's too late.

The Social Media Setup

Emily scrolled through her phone as Lily burst into laughter beside her.

"Oh my God, look at this," Lily snorted, typing furiously.

Emily glanced over. On Lily's screen was a fake gossip post about Jessica, a quiet girl in their class.

"Jessica's been caught sneaking into the boys' locker room," it read.

"It's just a joke," Lily smirked, adding a winking emoji.

Emily's stomach twisted. She had seen rumors destroy people— whispers in the hallway, stares in the cafeteria, ugly words scrawled on bathroom walls.

"What if someone did this to you?" Emily asked.

Lily shrugged, but her fingers hesitated over the screen.

"Seriously," Emily pressed. "This stuff spreads. You don't know what she's dealing with."

A long silence. Then Lily sighed and deleted the post.

The next day, Emily saw Jessica laughing with her friends, unaware of the disaster that almost unfolded. A wave of relief washed over Emily—one post, one moment of cruelty, could have ruined everything.

Moral:

A few clicks can ruin someone's life. Choose kindness over clout.

The Fight That Wasn't Worth It

Jordan's phone buzzed again. Another message. Another video.

Tony, his best friend, was being called out—humiliated in front of half the school.

"You gonna fight him?" someone texted.

Tony clenched his fists. His face was tight with anger. "What do I do?" he asked Jordan.

Jordan knew what people expected. They wanted a show. A fight in the hallway, fists flying, teachers scrambling to break it up.

But Jordan also knew something else—last week, a kid got expelled for fighting. Zero tolerance. It wasn't just about bruises and pride. It was about their futures.

"It's not worth it, man," Jordan said quietly.

Tony exhaled hard, shaking with frustration. But he listened. He turned and walked away.

The next morning, the principal announced new, harsher punishments for fighting. Jordan and Tony exchanged a look across the cafeteria.

It could've been them.

Moral:

Walking away from a fight is harder than throwing a punch—but it's always smarter.

The Vape Trick

Sophia's heart pounded as the vape pen passed to her.

"It's just water vapor," Mia giggled. "Seriously, it's nothing."

Sophia wasn't so sure. She'd read about kids landing in the hospital, about chemicals nobody talked about. She thought about her little brother, about how she promised to be a good example.

"Nah, I'm good," she said, forcing a smile.

Mia shrugged and took a long inhale, exhaling a cloud of mist that smelled oddly sweet. Sophia tried to look unaffected, but she could feel the pressure building.

Everyone was doing it. It was just one hit, right?

"Come on, Sophia. Don't be lame," Jake said, elbowing her gently. "You're not even gonna try it once?"

Sophia felt the heat rise in her chest. Her friends were pressuring her now. They all laughed, expecting her to cave in.

"Just one hit, then you'll see it's no big deal," Mia urged, waving the vape around like it was a toy.

Sophia's mind raced. She thought about the risks, about what could go wrong. What if she ended up like the kids she'd read about? But the fear of being excluded, the thought of being seen as the "boring one" haunted her.

"I don't know…" she muttered, staring down at her feet.

"You're acting like such a baby," Jake teased, giving her a playful shove. "What's the big deal? You won't even get hooked from one puff."

Sophia swallowed hard, but she shook her head. "I really don't want to."

But just as she thought she had made up her mind, the peer pressure hit harder. The group of friends all started nudging her, calling her out for being scared, for not fitting in.

"Everyone else is doing it, Sophia. Are you really gonna sit there and be that one person?" Mia pressed. "What, are you scared of a little vapor?"

It was too much. Sophia grabbed the vape, telling herself just one hit wouldn't hurt.

She raised it to her lips and took a quick puff. The cool vapor felt strange in her lungs, and she coughed uncontrollably. The taste was sickly sweet, and she immediately regretted it.

"See? No big deal," Mia said, but there was a hint of pride in her voice.

That night, just before bed, Sophia's phone buzzed. She looked down at a text from one of their other friends:

"Can you believe Jamie's in the ER? Apparently, the vape messed with her heart rate or something. She's been hooked up to a bunch of machines. They're saying it was a bad reaction to the chemicals in it.

Sophia's stomach dropped. She felt a cold sweat form on her forehead. That could have been her.

The next morning at school, word spread quickly. Everyone was talking about Jamie's hospitalization. Some whispered about how the doctors were concerned about long-term damage from vaping. Others were just focused on the drama of it all. Sophia couldn't shake the feeling that she had dodged a bullet, but at the same time, she was worried. Was Jamie okay?

When she saw Jamie later in the week, hooked up to an IV and looking pale, Sophia couldn't stop herself. She walked over to her.

"Jamie, are you alright?" she asked softly.

Jamie's eyes flickered with guilt. "I messed up, Sophia. I didn't think it'd hurt, but it did. I should've listened to you… you were right."

Sophia swallowed hard, fighting back tears. "I should've said no, too. I almost didn't."

Jamie smiled weakly. "It's hard when everyone's pressuring you. But we have to remember our health is more important than looking cool."

Sophia nodded, feeling a weight lift off her shoulders. That night, she texted Mia and Jake, explaining why she couldn't be a part of the group's vape sessions anymore. They didn't respond at first, but after a few days, they apologized. The group dynamics had shifted, but Sophia felt at peace with her decision.

Moral:

Just because everyone is doing it doesn't mean it's safe. Peer pressure is temporary, but your health and integrity last forever.

The Dangerous Dare

Dylan peered over the edge of the playground structure. It was at least ten feet down.

"Come on, don't be weak," Jake jeered. "It's not even that high."

Dylan's pulse hammered in his ears. It wasn't about the height—it was about the risk. One bad landing, one mistake, and he'd be spending months in a cast.

"This is dumb," he muttered, stepping back.

The others groaned, but they moved on.

A week later, someone else took the dare. The crack of bone against pavement still echoed in Dylan's head.

He had never been so glad to walk away.

Moral:

True strength is saying no when something feels wrong.

The Midnight Escape Plan

Leah's phone buzzed under her pillow.

"Yo, we're sneaking out. Don't be lame."

Leah sat up, chewing her lip. It sounded fun—kinda rebellious. But something felt off. She thought about her parents, how strict they were, and how disappointed they'd be if they found out she snuck out.

"Nah, I'm good," she typed back.

A minute later, another text came through. "Bruh, you're so boring. We were gonna hit up this party, but now you're just gonna stay in? Whatever. Don't hit us up later when you're mad you missed out."

Leah frowned. She didn't wanna be the odd one out, but she also didn't wanna mess up. She knew how her friends could be when they didn't get their way—salty and annoyed. But something still felt off.

"I'm staying home. You guys be safe," she replied.

The next morning, Leah woke up to a bunch of messages. She opened up the group chat and saw the chaos.

"Oh my God," Rachel typed. "We got caught! The cops brought us back home at like 2 a.m. My parents are so mad—they took my phone and grounded me for a month."

Leah blinked. She felt kinda relieved, but also bad for them. Then she saw more texts coming in.

"I can't believe we trusted Mia to drive," Olivia typed. "She's not even supposed to have the car, and now she's grounded for the rest of the semester. My parents are on my case too."

Leah was kinda glad she stayed home, but then Rachel hit her up in person at school.

"So you just stayed home last night, huh?" Rachel said, looking at Leah like she was annoyed. "Guess some people don't know how to have fun."

Leah shrugged. "I just wasn't feelin' it. Y'all could've gotten in real trouble."

Rachel rolled her eyes. "Yeah, whatever. I guess you're just perfect or something." She walked off, clearly still mad.

Leah was lowkey upset, but she figured it was just frustration talking. Later that day, Rachel texted her. "Yo, I'm sorry. I was acting dumb. I should've listened to you. Getting caught wasn't worth it."

Leah smiled, relieved. She didn't mind being the one to stay out of trouble.

Moral:

Don't let peer pressure mess with your judgment. It's better to chill and be safe than regret it later.

The Homework Hustle

Ethan stared at the crisp twenty-dollar bill.

"It's easy money," Jake grinned. "Just do my homework."

Ethan hesitated. It wasn't like stealing—it was just an assignment. But deep down, he knew it wasn't right.

"You should just ask for help instead," he said, pushing the money away.

Days later, the teacher found out about the cheating. Detentions were handed out. Ethan walked away with his integrity intact.

Moral:

Helping someone cheat isn't the same as helping them succeed.

The Shoplifting Scheme

Macy's stomach twisted as her friends snuck jewelry into their pockets.

"Come on, it's just earrings," they whispered.

Macy took a step back. "If you get caught, that's on you," she warned.

Minutes later, alarms blared. Security guards rushed forward.

Macy stood outside, watching the consequences unfold. She had never been more grateful for her instincts.

Moral:

If it feels wrong, don't do it.

The Reckless Selfie

Ryan and Jake had always chased the next thrill, the next viral moment. So when Jake spotted an old warehouse with a flat rooftop, he grinned.

"Come up here, man! The view's sick," Jake called as he scrambled up the rusted fire escape.

Ryan hesitated. The metal groaned under Jake's weight. "Dude, that's not safe."

Jake laughed. "Relax. One quick pic, then I'm down."

Ryan watched, heart pounding, as Jake edged toward the side. He stretched out his arm, angling his phone for the perfect shot.

Then—his foot slipped.

Ryan's breath caught. But at the last second, Jake caught the ledge, laughing it off. "See? No big deal."

A week later, Ryan scrolled through his feed and froze. News story. Same warehouse. Different kid.

Fatal fall.

Ryan's stomach dropped. That could've been Jake.

Moral:

No amount of likes is worth your life.

The Fake Gossip Game

Tasha's phone buzzed.

"Yo, did you hear about Mia?"

The group chat was blowing up with messages.

"She totally cheated on her boyfriend."

"She's a liar, bro."

"I heard she was talking to two dudes at once."

Tasha squinted at her screen, feeling her stomach churn. Mia? No way. That wasn't her. Mia was chill, kept to herself—not someone to do something like that.

"She didn't do that," Tasha typed quickly, hoping to shut it down before it went any further.

The chat paused for a second. Then someone hit her with a laughing emoji.

"C'mon, Tasha. It's just jokes."

Tasha's eyes flashed with frustration. This wasn't funny. She thought about Mia—how she would feel if people were spreading lies about her. "Would it be funny if it was about you?" Tasha snapped back.

Nothing for a minute. Then the chat started to slow down. People started to back off, but the damage had already been done.

The next day, Tasha spotted Mia walking down the hallway. She was looking down, scrolling through her phone. Her usual confident stride was gone—she looked like she was carrying the weight of the world.

Tasha's heart sank. Mia looked like she was about to break.

"Yo, Mia!" Tasha called out, hurrying over to her.

Mia looked up, eyes red, and her face drained of all energy.

"Hey," Tasha said, sitting down next to her. "I just wanna say... I'm sorry about all the stuff that's been going around. It's not true, right?"

Mia sighed, her shoulders dropping. "Nah, it's not true. I don't even know how it started. I've just been trying to ignore it, hoping it would go away."

Tasha frowned, guilt crawling up her spine. "I should've said something in the chat, Mia. I'm really sorry. You don't deserve this. None of it's true, and I'm here for you."

Mia gave her a weak smile, but it didn't reach her eyes. "Thanks, Tasha. I didn't think anyone would believe it... but it feels like everyone's been talking about it."

Tasha clenched her jaw. This was wrong. "Listen, I'm not gonna let people talk about you like that. You're not alone in this, okay? We're gonna get this straight."

Mia looked at her, her eyes still a little empty but thankful. "Thanks... I just don't know what to do. It's everywhere."

Tasha thought for a second. "Well, we can start by telling people the truth. This is crazy. I'm gonna talk to some of the others who've been spreading the rumors."

Later that day, Tasha went straight to a few of their friends who had been part of the gossip. She wasn't being shy about it. "Yo, what's the deal? Mia doesn't deserve this. It's straight-up messed up to talk about her like that. You gotta chill with that."

At first, a couple of them shrugged it off, but Tasha didn't back down. "Come on, think about it—what if it was your sister? You wouldn't want anyone spreading stuff like that about her. Just think before you talk next time, alright?"

Eventually, some of the others started backing off. They apologized and even helped to clear Mia's name, letting people know the rumors were just that—rumors. It didn't fix everything, but the pressure was starting to lift.

The next day at lunch, Mia sat with Tasha. Her shoulders were still tense, but she wasn't completely hiding from the world anymore.

"Thanks for having my back," Mia said quietly. "I don't know what I would've done without you."

"I got you, Mia," Tasha replied, smiling. "Friends don't let friends go through stuff alone. And this mess? We're fixing it, together."

Moral:

A rumor can ruin a life, but you have the power to stop it. Don't let a friend face that alone—speak up and show up.

The Energy Drink Disaster

Nick cracked open the can, the fizz loud in the quiet room.

"Bet you can't chug three," Jay dared, smirking.

Nick hesitated. He'd heard stories—kids getting heart palpitations, even collapsing. But his friends were watching.

"Come on, don't be weak."

His pride won. He downed the first. Then the second. By the third, his hands shook.

His chest felt... tight. His heart pounded like a drum.

"Dude, you good?"

Nick's vision blurred. He stood, but the room tilted. The last thing he heard was someone yelling his name before everything went black.

Hours later, he woke in a hospital bed, his mom crying beside him.

The doctor shook his head. "You're lucky. Some kids don't get a second chance."

Moral:

Just because it's sold in stores doesn't mean it's safe in excess.

The Street Race Regret

Jay's fingers hovered over the ignition, heart pounding. The street ahead was dark and quiet, just the sound of engines revving and tires skidding on the asphalt. Streetlights blinked on like a countdown to what he knew would be a race of no return.

Mark leaned over with a smirk, glancing at Jay's Mustang. "Yo, I bet I can beat you easy, bro. You in?"

Jay's foot twitched on the gas pedal. His pulse was racing just as fast as the engine. The familiar excitement of the race, the feeling of power and control, it was all right there in front of him.

But then, something hit him. Headlines flashed through his mind: Teen driver loses control. Fatal crash. He froze for a second, gripping the steering wheel tight. This wasn't a game. This was real life, and he wasn't sure he was ready to risk it all for a stupid race.

Mark wasn't waiting. "Come on, man, don't be soft. You're gonna let me show you up?" He revved his engine, making Jay flinch. The pressure was on. His friends were already cheering him on from the sidewalk. His reputation—everything he'd worked for in the crew—was on the line. But something deep inside him screamed that this wasn't the way to go.

Jay shook his head, finally finding his voice. "Nah, man. Not worth it."

Mark shot him a look. "You serious, bro? Don't tell me you're scared."

"I'm not scared. I just… I got more to lose than some race, Mark," Jay said, his voice steady, though his insides were all over the place. He could feel the weight of his decision in his chest, but it felt right.

Mark just rolled his eyes. "Whatever, bro. Don't be lame." He slammed the gas, tires screeching as his car tore off down the street.

Jay watched for a moment, his grip still tight on the steering wheel, then turned his key off and leaned back in his seat, staring at the dark stretch of road. He couldn't ignore the feeling in his gut. The rush? Yeah, it was there, but the thought of something going wrong, of hurting someone, or even worse—hurting himself—was heavier than any race he could win.

That night, Jay's phone buzzed with a news alert. His thumb hesitated over the screen as he opened it.

"Street racer crashes into tree. Passenger injured."

Jay's stomach dropped. His hands went cold as he read the details. Mark's car—his buddy—was in the crash. His stomach twisted in knots. That could've been him. That should've been him.

He sat in the car for a long time, staring at the empty road, the adrenaline from earlier fading away. The whole crew had been hyping up the race, but none of them knew what Jay had been thinking when he'd pulled back. None of them knew the panic that hit him right before they'd started. He wasn't trying to be a hero, but in that moment, Jay had realized there was more to life than winning a race or showing off.

His phone buzzed again. It was Mark texting him. Yo, bro, I messed up. I shouldn't have pushed you to race. I'm glad you didn't go through with it. You saved me from a stupid mistake.

Jay stared at the screen for a minute, then typed back. Yeah, man. Glad I did too. Let's slow down, alright? We've got more to live for than just racing.

Mark's reply came almost instantly. Facts, bro. I'm sorry. I'll chill.

Jay sighed and leaned back, the weight of everything sinking in. Sometimes, it wasn't about proving yourself or living up to some expectation. It was about taking care of yourself and being smart enough to step back when the pressure was too much.

Moral:

Don't make "crash dummy" decisions that could put your life in danger.

The Peer Pressure Prank

"Let's prank-call Mrs. Dawson," Tyler whispered, grinning. "It'll be hilarious."

Brandon hesitated. Their history teacher was strict, sure—but this felt wrong.

"Relax," Tyler said. "She'll never know it's us."

Brandon swallowed as Tyler dialed, disguising his voice. "Hello, is this the math teacher? Because you sure add a lot of homework."

Laughter erupted.

But then—

"Call traced," a robotic voice said.

Panic.

The next day, the principal pulled them aside. Mrs. Dawson wasn't just mad—she looked disappointed.

Brandon wished he had walked away.

Moral:

If you have to hide it, you probably shouldn't do it.

The Locker Room Leak

Aiden's friend nudged him. "Dude, let's record Jason changing. It'll be funny."

Aiden's stomach twisted. "That's messed up."

"Relax," his friend smirked. "Just a joke."

Aiden swatted the phone away.

The next day, the school was in chaos. Someone else had filmed—and got caught. Expelled.

Jason's eyes were red-rimmed, humiliated.

Aiden felt a wave of relief. He hadn't been part of it.

But guilt gnawed at him—because he could've stopped it from happening at all.

Moral:

Privacy isn't a joke. Protect it.

The Overworked Athlete

Jasmine's knee throbbed with every step she took down the court. The sharp pain was back, just like the day before. She tried to push through it, but it was different this time. It wasn't just the usual ache after practice. This felt deeper—worse.

"Shake it off, Jasmine!" Coach snapped, his voice sharp like a whistle. "You're fine. We need you out there."

Jasmine bit her lip, trying not to let the tears well up. Her knee felt like it was about to give out. Just a little longer, just finish the game, she thought, but the pain was already too much.

"Coach, I don't think I can—" she started, but the words didn't come out right.

"Come on, just play through it! We need this win," Coach urged, looking at her with a mix of frustration and desperation.

Jasmine hesitated. Her teammates were depending on her. But she remembered the stories—athletes who pushed too hard, too fast, and ended up with injuries that cost them their careers. She didn't want to be one of those stories.

But then her friend, Mia, called out from the sidelines, "Jas, you've got this. Push through, it's just a little pain."

Jasmine hesitated for a moment longer, then took a deep breath. "Yeah, okay, I'll try," she lied, forcing herself back into the game.

As she played, the pain intensified with every pivot and every jump. Her knee felt like it was on fire, but she didn't want to disappoint anyone. She kept going, trying to ignore the ache, but every time she moved, it screamed louder in her mind.

This isn't worth it, she thought, I can't keep going like this.

The game ended, and Jasmine limped off the court, trying to act like everything was fine. But the pain was worse than before.

The next morning, as she limped into the locker room, her coach was waiting for her. He looked at her with a raised brow. "Jasmine, what's up? You looked a little off yesterday."

She winced as she sat down on the bench. Her knee was swollen now, more than it had been before. She couldn't hide it any longer. "Coach, I gotta sit out for a while. My knee's messed up."

Coach frowned, eyes narrowing in concern. "You sure? We've got the championship game coming up, and I need you out there."

"I know, but I can't keep pushing it," Jasmine said, her voice firm despite the uncertainty swirling in her stomach. "I've been playing through pain for weeks, but this is too much. I don't want to make it worse."

There was a long silence as Coach stared at her, the pressure of the season weighing heavily on both of them. Finally, he nodded. "Alright, sit this one out. But I need you to get it checked out. We'll figure out a plan."

Jasmine's relief was almost overwhelming. For the first time in weeks, she felt like she was actually taking control of her health instead of ignoring it for the sake of a game.

That night, during the game she would've been playing in, Jasmine's phone buzzed with a text from Mia.

You won't believe this... Jamie collapsed during the second half. Torn ligament. Her season's over.

Jasmine's heart sank. She felt guilty for not being there for her team, but at the same time, she was grateful she had listened to her body. She didn't want to risk ending up like Jamie.

The next morning, she called her coach to update him. "I'm glad you decided to sit out, Jasmine. Jamie's injury could've been avoided if she had done the same."

Jasmine nodded, relieved. "I'll be back stronger, Coach. I promise. But I need to take care of this knee first."

Moral:

Listen to your body, not just the pressure.

The Prescription Pills Trap

Zach stared at the small, white pill in his friend's hand. His friend, Jason, held it out like it was something normal—just another way to feel better. The way Jason was acting, you'd think it was just an Advil or something. But something about it didn't sit right with Zach.

"Come on, bro, just take it. It helps with stress," Jason said, his voice casual, like it was no big deal.

Zach shifted uncomfortably, eyeing the pill. "Where'd you get it?" He had a bad feeling in his gut, but he didn't want to sound paranoid.

Jason shrugged, his grin wide and carefree. "Don't worry about it, man. You need it. Trust me."

Zach's mind raced. He could feel the pressure building—Jason was his friend, right? They'd been through everything together. But this was different. The pill wasn't something you could just pop without consequences.

His heart pounded as he stared at the pill, the urge to just take it and calm his nerves for once fighting with the little voice in his head telling him to walk away. What if it really does help? He thought. What if I just take it this one time?

Jason leaned in, a little more forceful this time. "Come on, Zac, everyone's doing it. It's no big deal."

Zach's hand reached out. He almost took it. His fingers brushed the smooth surface of the pill. Just a quick fix, he thought. One pill, one time. It's not gonna hurt me.

But just as he was about to pop it into his mouth, a cold shiver ran down his spine. His gut twisted even harder. What if this isn't what it seems? What if it's something worse?

He froze.

He pulled his hand back, dropping the pill. "Nah, I'm good," he said, trying to sound calm, though his voice cracked a little. "I don't need it."

Jason rolled his eyes, frustrated. "Come on, bro. You're lame. It's just to take the edge off. You'd feel so much better."

Zach shook his head, taking a step back. "Nah. I don't need to mess with that."

Jason scoffed, walking away with a muttered, "Whatever, man."

Zach watched him leave, still feeling the weight of the decision he almost made. But deep down, he was relieved he'd stopped himself.

Days passed. Zach couldn't shake the feeling of unease, but he tried to push it out of his mind. That was until the text came through that night.

It was from one of their mutual friends. Jason's in the ER. He almost didn't make it.

Zach's heart sank as he read the next message: The pill was laced with fentanyl.

His hands shook as he dropped his phone onto his bed. He couldn't believe it. Jason could've died—over one stupid decision. Zach's mind replayed the moment he almost took that pill, the way he almost convinced himself it'd be fine. But now, he knew it wasn't just a random pill. It could've been the end.

Zach took a deep breath, thankful that he had stopped in time. He couldn't help but feel sick to his stomach. That could've been me.

Moral:

Never take pills that aren't prescribed to you.

The Relationship Red Flag

Sarah heard shouting.

Her best friend, Paige, was near tears as her boyfriend grabbed her wrist. "I said I was sorry!"

Sarah's chest tightened. This wasn't normal.

"Hey," she said firmly. "Let's go."

Later, Paige sighed. "He doesn't mean it. He's just stressed."

Sarah took her hand. "That's not love."

It took time, but Paige finally left him.

Moral:

Speak up when you see unhealthy relationships.

The Online Stranger

Mark sat on the couch, scrolling through his phone when his friend, Tessa, leaned over with a wide grin on her face. "Check him out," she said, waving her phone in front of him. "His name's Jason. He's so cool. We should totally meet up."

Mark glanced at the phone, half-interested but mostly skeptical. He didn't know this "Jason" from anywhere. "You don't even know him," he said, trying to keep his voice calm. "He could be anyone."

Tessa waved him off, laughing. "It's fine, Mark. He's super chill. He told me we could hang out this weekend. You're just being paranoid."

Mark's stomach dropped as he watched her scroll through their conversations on social media. Jason seemed sweet enough on the surface—funny, easy to talk to, always complimenting her. But something about it didn't sit right with Mark. They didn't even know the guy's real name, and the photos he sent her were all posed and carefully edited.

"You sure about this?" Mark asked, his brow furrowed. "You don't even know what he looks like in real life. And he could be lying about everything."

Tessa shrugged, clearly not taking it seriously. "Relax. You worry too much."

A week later, Mark's phone buzzed. It was Tessa, calling. His gut immediately told him something was wrong. "What's up?" he answered, trying to keep his tone steady.

Her voice shook, cracking slightly with fear. "Mark... he lied about his age. He's way older than he said he was. Like, way older. And, like, I don't know what to do. I told him I wasn't comfortable meeting up, but he's being really pushy."

Mark's heart sank. "I told you to be careful," he muttered, his hands clenching into fists. "You shouldn't have even thought about meeting him in the first place."

"I know, I know," Tessa said, her voice barely above a whisper. "But he seemed so nice, and he made me feel so special. He was all, 'Don't worry, I'm not like the other guys.'"

"Listen, Tessa, you need to cut this off right now," Mark said, his voice sharp.

"You've gotta block him. Like, right now."

Tessa hesitated. "But—what if he's mad? What if he starts, like, threatening me or something?"

Mark could feel the panic rising in her voice. "Don't worry about that. You block him, and I'll help you report him. No one gets away with that crap."

Tessa finally agreed, and she blocked Jason from all her social media accounts. But that night, Mark couldn't shake the feeling that something still wasn't right. He stayed up late, staring at his phone, hoping she'd be okay.

The next morning, Tessa texted him with an update.

"He found a way to message me from another account," she wrote. "But I told my parents, and they called the cops. They traced his IP address, and they're investigating him. He's been arrested, Mark. He's been lying about his identity for months."

Mark's heart pounded. He felt a mix of relief and disgust. "Thank God you told your parents. That could've gone way worse."

"Yeah," Tessa texted back. "I'm just glad I didn't go to meet him. He's, like, way older than he said. I don't know what he would've done if I showed up."

Mark exhaled, feeling a heavy weight lift off his chest. "You did the right thing. I'm proud of you. I know it wasn't easy, but you stepped up. And you don't have to deal with that creep anymore."

Tessa sent a simple text back: "Thanks. I don't think I'll ever trust someone online the same way again."

Mark smiled, even though he was still shaken. "Lesson learned."

Moral:

Not everyone online is who they say they are. Stay safe and trust your instincts.

The Body-Shaming Comments

Lena's friends giggled. "Look at her outfit. Yikes."

They nudged Lena. "Say something funny."

She looked at the girl—head down, arms crossed, shrinking under their words.

Lena took a breath. "No. That's not cool."

Her friends rolled their eyes.

But later, the girl whispered, "Thanks."

Moral:

Kindness is always the right choice.

The College Party Wake-Up Call

"Come on, Ben. No one will check IDs."

Ben eyed the party. Loud music. Red cups.

*His gut screamed **bad idea.***

"I'm good," he said.

The next morning, headlines flashed across his screen.

Police raid underage drinking party. Arrests made.

Ben exhaled. Dodged a bullet.

Moral:

Just because you can, doesn't mean you should.

The Skipping Class Trap

Ava's friends were relentless. "Come on, Ava, one class won't kill you," Jasmine coaxed. "We'll just grab fries and chill. You'll catch up later."

Ava hesitated. Math wasn't her strongest subject, but the idea of missing class—just once—seemed harmless. So she followed them out the side doors and into the warm afternoon air. At the fast-food place, they laughed, snapped selfies, and for a while, she felt free.

But the next day, Ava's stomach twisted as she sat down for the quiz. She scanned the first problem. Then the second. Her heart pounded. She had no idea how to solve them.

Her friends managed to scrape by with barely passing grades. Ava? She failed. And worse, the material would be on the final exam.

She clenched her fists under the desk. "Never again," she whispered.

Moral:

Missing one class can set you back more than you think.

The Fight Instigator

Marcus could feel his friends' eyes on him, their voices hyping him up. "You gotta show them you're not weak," Derek said, nudging his shoulder.

Across the courtyard, another group of guys stood, smirking. Marcus felt his blood boil. His heart pounded in his chest. Every muscle in his body screamed at him to walk away—but the pressure was suffocating.

Before he could think, he swung.

The next thing he knew, hands were yanking him back. A teacher's voice cut through the shouts.

Minutes later, he sat in the principal's office, his knuckles bruised, his stomach twisted in regret. Three days of suspension. A mark on his record.

All for what? To impress people who didn't care about his future?

Moral:

The one who starts the fight is usually the one who regrets it.

The Inappropriate Picture Request

Taylor sat on her bed, scrolling through her messages. Her phone buzzed again—this time from Ryan, her boyfriend. She smiled at first. But then, her smile faded when she saw the picture attached to his message.

"Just between us," it read, with a picture she never expected to see. Taylor's stomach dropped. She stared at the image for a moment, feeling a cold chill run through her. Her breath caught in her chest, and her hands went clammy.

"Come on, just one picture," Ryan messaged again. "No one else will see. I swear."

Taylor's mind was racing. Her heart pounded in her ears. The alarms in her brain went off like sirens. She knew where this could go. If she sent something, it wouldn't be just between them. What if they broke up? What if he showed his friends? The idea of something so personal being out of her control was terrifying.

She quickly typed back, her fingers trembling, "Not happening."

Ryan's reply came almost immediately. "You're being dramatic. It's not a big deal. You know I'll never show anyone."

Taylor frowned. She could feel the pressure building, like he was trying to convince her. "It is a big deal, Ryan. It's not about you showing anyone, it's about trust. I don't feel comfortable with that."

He responded with a bunch of laughing emojis. "You're just overthinking it. Trust me, no one will ever know."

Taylor stared at the screen, anger bubbling up. She had tried to be nice about it, but now he was being persistent. It was like he didn't care about her feelings, or her boundaries.

"Honestly, I'm not trying to be a prude. But this just feels off," she typed, trying to keep her cool.

"Wow, really?" Ryan replied. "Fine, be that way. I thought you trusted me, but I guess not."

Taylor bit her lip. She had tried to be patient, but now she was just irritated. She had been with Ryan for a few months, but the way he was pressuring her made her feel like he didn't respect her. If this was what he wanted, it wasn't worth it. She wasn't going to let him manipulate her into doing something she wasn't comfortable with.

"Look, Ryan," she finally typed, her hands shaking with a mix of frustration and relief. "You're not hearing me. I'm not doing it, and you need to understand that. And if you can't, then maybe we shouldn't be together."

Ryan's response was instant. "Seriously? You're going to break up with me over this? Whatever, Taylor. You're so dramatic."

Taylor stared at his message for a long moment. She knew what she had to do, even if it wasn't easy. She took a deep breath and typed her final message:

"Yeah, I am. I'm done. I don't need someone who can't respect me."

Before Ryan could respond, she hit send and tossed her phone onto her bed, feeling a rush of emotions—relief, disappointment, but most of all, pride. She had stood up for herself.

A month later, the school hallways buzzed with whispers. Taylor overheard a group of girls talking in the locker room. "Did you hear? Someone's private pictures leaked. That same boy, Ryan? He's at the center of the scandal."

Taylor froze. Her stomach dropped, and her heart raced. She quickly walked away, her mind spinning. She knew exactly what had happened. It had been just as she feared. Ryan had pressured someone else into sending pictures, and now they were everywhere.

Taylor hugged her arms tightly to her chest, the weight of the situation sinking in. Relief washed over her as she realized she had made the right choice. She had been so close to being a part of that mess.

Later that day, she texted her best friend, Emily. "I'm so glad I didn't give in. I could've been a part of that, and I would've never been able to take it back."

Emily responded almost instantly. "You were so smart. Once you send something, you lose control of it forever. Good thing you stood your ground."

Taylor smiled as she read the message. It felt good to know she wasn't alone in understanding the weight of her decision. She had chosen to protect her dignity and her future, no matter what.

Moral:

Once you send a picture, you lose control of it forever. Always protect your boundaries.

The Disrespectful Outburst

Jaden sat in class, his pencil tapping against the desk as he tried to focus. His teacher's voice kept echoing in the background, reminding him to stay on task. He wasn't really listening to her, though. His mind was elsewhere, replaying last night's basketball game and the stupid mistake he made with a last-second shot.

"Jaden, focus," she said again, glancing over at his half-finished notes.

His friends snickered quietly. "She's always on you, bro," Malik whispered, nudging him with his elbow.

Jaden's frustration started to build. Why did she always pick on him? He wasn't the only one who zoned out sometimes. Why didn't she give him a break?

The teacher called him out again. "Jaden, your notes are incomplete. You're falling behind."

That was it. Jaden snapped. He could feel his face go red, his heart pounding. He shot a glance at his friends, who were now watching the situation unfold like it was some kind of reality show.

"Whatever Bro, just shut up talking to me!" Jaden blurted out; his voice louder than he intended.

There was a moment of silence. The entire class froze, staring at him. Jaden's chest tightened, and the words hit him like a punch in the gut the second they left his mouth. His teacher's face didn't flinch; it hardened, her jaw tight, but her eyes... her eyes told a different story. There was a flicker of hurt, just enough for Jaden to notice. He immediately regretted it, but it was too late.

The teacher didn't say anything for a few seconds. The tension was thick. Then, calmly, she said, "Detention. After school. And I'm calling your parents."

The class murmured, and Jaden slumped in his seat, feeling the weight of his mistake. The rest of the period passed by in a blur. He barely heard anything the teacher said, too caught up in the knot in his stomach.

When the bell rang, Jaden walked out with Malik and the others, but his mind was elsewhere. His friends were talking, but he wasn't listening. All he could think about was how he messed up. The worst part wasn't the detention or the call home. It was the way his teacher had looked at him. The trust he'd taken for granted was gone now. She wasn't going to call on him anymore, wasn't going to give him that same benefit of the doubt.

That evening, as he sat in his room, Jaden couldn't stop thinking about it. He replayed the entire scene over and over in his head. The words he'd said. The look in her eyes. The embarrassment he felt now.

His phone buzzed, and he saw a text from Malik: "Yo, that was wild today. But don't sweat it. You'll be good."

Jaden stared at the screen for a long moment before typing back, "Nah, man. I messed up. I shouldn't have said that. I feel like crap about it."

The next morning, as he walked into class, he felt the weight of the tension in the air. His teacher was at the front, but she didn't look at him. She was focused on the board, as if he didn't exist. That hurt more than anything.

He sat down, trying to focus, but all he could think about was how he had disrespected her. He finally couldn't take it anymore.

During a break, he stood up and walked to the front of the classroom. His teacher looked up, surprised.

"Ms. Carter," Jaden started, his voice a little shaky, "I just... I wanted to say I'm sorry. I really messed up yesterday. I didn't mean to say that to you. I've been frustrated, but that's no excuse. You didn't deserve that. I was out of line, and I just wanted to say I regret it."

There was a long pause, and Jaden held his breath, waiting for her response. Finally, she nodded slowly.

"I appreciate you saying that, Jaden. Apology accepted," she said, her voice soft but firm. "I know you're better than that. Just... remember next time that words matter. They can't be taken back."

Jaden nodded, feeling a little better, but also realizing how much work he still had to do to rebuild that trust.

He walked back to his seat, and Malik gave him a quick thumbs-up. He could feel a small sense of relief. The class didn't feel as tense anymore, but Jaden knew he had a long way to go to earn back the respect he'd lost.

The bell rang, and Jaden walked out, feeling like he had learned something important. Respect wasn't automatic. It had to be earned, and once it was lost, it wasn't easy to get back.

Moral:

Disrespect won't get you ahead—self-control will.

The Shoplifting Pressure

Maya's fingers brushed the tiny necklace on the store shelf. "Come on," Tia whispered. "Just slip it in your pocket. No one will notice."

Maya's heart pounded. The cashier was busy. The cameras weren't pointed their way.

She felt a rush of nerves and excitement—until she thought about what would happen if she got caught. Security. Handcuffs. Her parents' faces if they got that call.

She shook her head. "Nah, I'm good."

Tia rolled her eyes, but Maya didn't care. Later, she watched from across the mall as security pulled Tia aside.

Moral:

If they push you to steal, they're not your real friends.

The Vaping Experiment

Cameron coughed as the thick vapor swirled in front of him, the sweet scent of strawberry filling the air. Alex grinned, holding out the vape pen like it was the coolest thing ever.

"Come on, bro, just try it," Alex said, raising an eyebrow. "It's literally not even that bad for you."

Cameron hesitated. He'd seen the ads. He'd read the articles. He knew what vaping really did to your body. But everyone around him was doing it. He didn't want to be that guy—the one who didn't fit in.

He reached for the vape, but then stopped short. He thought about his cousin, who'd ended up in the hospital after vaping way too much. And his track coach, who had just given them a whole speech about how vaping could totally mess with your lungs. He was trying to get faster for the next race—he couldn't let something stupid like this mess up his training.

Cameron exhaled sharply, trying to shake off the urge. "Nah, I'm good," he said, pulling his hand back.

Alex rolled his eyes. "Dude, you're being mad lame. It's just a little puff. Stop acting like it's a big deal." He laughed and took another hit, blowing out a cloud of smoke that made Cameron's throat tighten.

Cameron stood there for a second, watching his friends, but something didn't feel right. He couldn't let this be him. He thought about the people who'd gotten caught up in it—how quickly vaping went from 'just something fun to try' to an addiction, how people's lungs were getting wrecked. He didn't want to end up in the ER, breathing like he'd just ran a marathon... every single day.

A few weeks later, Cameron was walking up the stairs at school when he saw Alex at the bottom, gasping for air. He had a hand on the railing, trying to steady himself.

"Yo, Alex, you good?" Cameron asked, eyebrow raised. He was honestly a little freaked out. Alex wasn't even that out of shape.

Alex looked up, his face pale, and wiped sweat from his forehead. "Nah, man... I'm not good," he panted, breathing hard. "I went to the doctor yesterday. They said my lungs are messed up. The vaping... it did some serious damage. I can't even walk up the stairs without feeling like I'm gonna pass out."

Cameron's heart dropped. He froze, processing what Alex was saying. It hit him hard—this wasn't just some rumor. Alex's body was actually feeling the effects of something he thought was no big deal.

"Dude, I'm sorry," Cameron said, his voice low. He wanted to say more, but he didn't know what to say. "I'm just glad I didn't—"

"Yeah, I get it," Alex cut him off, still gasping for air. "I thought I was invincible, you know? I thought it was just something everyone does. But now I'm paying for it. Don't make my mistake, Cam. It's not worth it."

Cameron nodded, his stomach twisting. He knew he had made the right choice, but hearing Alex say it like this made it real. He felt lucky, like he dodged a bullet, but at the same time, he couldn't help but feel bad for his friend.

"I won't, bro," Cameron said quietly, his eyes focused on Alex. "You got this. Just take care of yourself."

Moral:

Just because it's trendy doesn't mean it's safe. Don't risk your health for a little temporary satisfaction. You never know how bad it could get.

The Bullying Crossroad

Laughter rippled through the lunch table, light and careless, like pebbles skipping across water. Samantha felt its sharp edge before she even knew why.

"Look at his shoes," Bella giggled, flicking a french fry onto her tray. "Are those plastic?"

Samantha glanced at Kevin, sitting alone at the end of the cafeteria. His shoulders were hunched, eyes glued to his tray. His shoes—worn, scuffed, and slightly too big—peeked out beneath the table. A blush crept up his neck, but he didn't look up.

Bella nudged Samantha with a mischievous grin. "Come on, say something funny."

The words hung in the air like a dare. Samantha's throat tightened. She'd seen this play before—she'd either been the one being made fun of or the one quietly watching. And every time, she felt that same uncomfortable knot in her stomach.

She glanced back at Kevin, who hadn't moved, his fingers gripping his sandwich like he was trying to hold on to something that could keep him from disappearing.

Samantha's pulse hammered. She didn't want to be a part of this. Not anymore.

"This isn't cool," she said, her voice low but clear.

The table went quiet, the sound of trays scraping against tables taking over. Bella's eyes flickered with surprise before narrowing. "It's just a joke," she muttered, rolling her eyes. But Samantha saw the shift—people stopped laughing, stopped looking at Kevin and instead looked down at their trays, shifting in their seats, pretending to be interested in whatever they were eating.

Kevin's head lifted slightly, his gaze slowly meeting hers. For a moment, he didn't say anything. He just stared, his eyes wide, like he couldn't believe she'd actually spoken up. Then, in the smallest of gestures, he gave her a quick nod. Not a smile, but something like gratitude.

That was enough for Samantha. She wasn't going to let this slide anymore.

The next day, as she sat at lunch with her friends, she felt a twinge of irritation when she saw Kevin sitting alone again. Bella, of course, was talking loudly about how she couldn't find her favorite hoodie, but Samantha couldn't shake the feeling that they were all acting like it was just another normal day.

She stood up. Without a second thought, she grabbed her tray and walked straight to where Kevin sat, his head down, eyes focused on his lunch like he was trying to be invisible.

Kevin looked up, clearly surprised. "Hey," Samantha said, trying to sound casual. "Mind if I sit here?"

Kevin blinked, clearly not expecting her to be the one to sit down with him. "Uh, sure," he stammered, scooting over to make room for her. He didn't say much more, but she noticed a hint of relief in his eyes.

The quiet between them felt strange, but Samantha wasn't bothered by it. She wasn't here to chat or make small talk. She was here because it felt like the right thing to do.

As she sat down, she glanced over at her table of friends. They were staring, eyes wide, mouths slightly open. Bella shot her a look, her expression one of disbelief.

"Seriously?" Bella said, her tone dripping with sarcasm. "You're gonna sit with him? Why?"

Samantha met her gaze without flinching. "Because you guys are being jerks, and someone needs to stop it."

Bella scoffed, but didn't argue. She just rolled her eyes and went back to gossiping with the others.

The rest of lunch passed by in silence, but it wasn't uncomfortable. It was... peaceful, in a way. Kevin didn't talk much, but he didn't need to. Just the fact that Samantha had sat with him made everything feel a little more okay.

The next day, Kevin caught her eye across the hallway. His lips curled up slightly, just enough to show he was thankful. And this time, Samantha smiled back.

It wasn't some huge victory, but it mattered. Because sometimes, standing up wasn't about making a scene or getting everyone's attention. Sometimes, it was about one small act of kindness. Sometimes, it was about sitting with someone who needed it, even when your friends were too busy being rude.

Samantha didn't need applause. She didn't need a speech. She just needed to know that she'd done the right thing.

Moral:

Silence supports the bully. Speaking up supports the victim. Even small acts of courage can change someone's day—and maybe even their life.

The Cheat Sheet Mistake

Noah's palms were sweaty as his friend slid the tiny paper under the desk. "Just look if you get stuck," he whispered.

The test started. Noah's heart pounded. The temptation was unbearable.

Then—Ms. Carter's voice. "David, come with me."

Noah turned in time to see his friend pale as the teacher held up the cheat sheet. A zero. A write-up. Possibly worse.

Noah let out a shaky breath. He had almost made the same mistake.

Moral:

Cheating might get you through one test, but it won't help you in life.

The Little White Lie

Emma's stomach churned as she clicked "send" on the email. "I couldn't finish my project. My grandma was really sick."

It wasn't even true. Sure, her grandma had been a little under the weather, but she was fine. Emma just couldn't bear the thought of turning in her half-done project, so she thought this excuse would buy her a little more time.

Her teacher, Ms. Carter, replied quickly. "I hope she's okay. Don't worry, we'll talk about the project when you're ready."

Emma felt a quick rush of relief. The lie had worked. She sat back in her chair, feeling the weight lift off her shoulders. But as the words flashed across the screen, she couldn't help but feel a little bit guilty.

The next day, her mom's voice broke through her thoughts as she walked into the kitchen. "Why did Ms. Carter ask how Grandma was doing?"

Emma froze, her heart racing. She had no idea how her mom found out, but the expression on her face said it all—she knew.

Emma's mind scrambled for an excuse, but it was too late. "I... I don't know. I guess she was just being nice," Emma stammered, but even as the words left her mouth, she knew it didn't make sense.

Her mom's eyes narrowed, her tone soft but stern. "Emma, you told me Grandma was fine. Why did you lie about it?"

"I... I just didn't want to turn the project in late," Emma admitted, her voice barely above a whisper. "I was embarrassed. I didn't finish it in time."

Her mom shook her head, a look of disappointment crossing her face. "I understand being nervous about a project, but lying isn't the way to handle it. That's not how we do things."

Emma's stomach sank, and she avoided her mom's gaze. "I'm sorry, Mom."

Later that afternoon, as Emma walked into school, she couldn't shake the feeling that something had changed. Ms. Carter had always been kind to her, but now every time Emma turned in an assignment or answered a question, Ms. Carter's eyes seemed to linger a little too long on her, as if deciding whether she should believe her or not. The trust between them had shifted, and Emma felt it.

During class, Ms. Carter asked the students to turn in their projects. When it was Emma's turn, she handed hers in with a quick, nervous glance. Ms. Carter paused, looking at her with an unreadable expression before saying, "Good job, Emma. I'm glad you got it done."

Emma nodded quickly, but the words felt hollow. She could feel her teacher's skepticism, even though Ms. Carter said nothing.

Later that week, when Emma wasn't feeling well, she almost didn't go to school. But the thought of making up another excuse filled her with dread. What if Ms. Carter didn't believe her? What if the lie had already cost her too much?

By the end of the week, Emma's anxiety had built up. She could no longer ignore the fact that every time Ms. Carter talked to her, she felt like her teacher was watching, waiting for Emma to slip up again.

The next day after class, Emma stayed behind. She stood awkwardly by Ms. Carter's desk, unsure of what to say.

"Is everything okay, Emma?" Ms. Carter asked kindly, but Emma could hear the underlying concern in her voice.

Emma swallowed hard, her hands twisting in front of her. "I just... I just want to say that I'm sorry for lying about my grandma. It was wrong, and I regret doing it. I didn't mean to make you doubt me."

Ms. Carter smiled gently, but there was a sadness in her eyes. "I appreciate your honesty, Emma. That's what matters now. But remember, trust takes time to rebuild. It's not something you can get back with just one apology."

Emma nodded, a lump forming in her throat. She knew she had learned the hard way that a lie might get you out of a tight spot, but it could cost you far more in the end—your reputation, your relationships, and your peace of mind.

From then on, Emma was more careful with her words. She worked harder to turn in her assignments on time, and when she had trouble, she owned up to it instead of hiding behind excuses.

But the lesson had already been learned: once trust is lost, it's much harder to regain.

Moral:

A lie might save you in the moment, but it can cost you in the long run. Trust, once broken, is hard to rebuild.

The Peer Pressure to Go Too Far

Kayla pulled her hoodie tighter around herself as she sat on the edge of Jason's bed, her fingers tangled together in her lap. The dim glow of his bedside lamp flickered, casting long shadows across the walls. Outside, the rain pattered lightly against the window, but inside, the air was thick—too thick, pressing against her chest like a weight she couldn't shake.

Jason sat beside her, his leg bouncing restlessly. He reached for her hand, his fingers tracing slow circles over her knuckles. "Babe," he murmured, his voice smooth, persuasive. "We've been together for months. Don't you think it's time?"

Kayla's stomach twisted. They'd had this conversation before—too many times. At first, it had been little comments, jokes mixed with soft smiles. Then it turned into late-night texts, the "if you love me" messages. And now, here they were again, his arm draped around her, his breath warm against her ear, whispering words that felt more like chains than love.

She hesitated. "Jason... I told you. I'm not ready."

His hand tightened around hers. "It's not a big deal, Kayla. Everyone does it."

She pulled away, standing up so fast that her knee bumped against the wooden nightstand. "That doesn't mean I have to," she shot back, her voice steadier than she felt.

Jason exhaled sharply, shaking his head. "Come on, Kay. Just once. It'll bring us closer."

Her pulse pounded in her ears. She wanted to believe him—to believe that love meant giving in, that saying yes would keep him from looking at her with that growing frustration in his eyes. But deep down, she knew—love wasn't supposed to feel like pressure.

Kayla swallowed hard, ignoring the way her hands trembled at her sides. "No," she said, louder this time.

Jason's expression darkened, his jaw clenching. For a second, she thought he'd argue, try to charm her into changing her mind like he always did. But instead, he let out a low scoff.

"Whatever," he muttered, rolling onto his side and grabbing his phone. The glow of the screen reflected off his face, already distracted, already somewhere else.

Kayla stared at him, her chest tight, her throat burning. She had spent so much time convincing herself that Jason's love was worth something—that his affection was proof of her worth. But in that moment, watching him shut her out so easily, she realized something: Love shouldn't make her feel small. Love shouldn't make her feel scared.

She turned toward the door, her heartbeat steadying with every step she took away from him.

One Week Later

Kayla stood by her locker, shoving her textbooks inside when she caught whispers from a group of girls nearby.

"Did you hear about Jason?" one of them said, giggling. "He's been talking to Brianna now."

"Yeah," another added. "Same old stuff. 'If you love me, you would.'"

Kayla's stomach twisted—not with jealousy, but with relief. That could have been her. That almost was her.

She straightened, exhaling a breath she hadn't realized she was holding. As she walked past Jason in the hallway, he glanced at her, as if expecting her to react. Maybe to be hurt. Maybe to come crawling back.

She didn't give him the satisfaction. She walked past without a glance, her head held high, knowing she had made the right choice.

Moral:

If they really love you, they won't pressure you.

The Loaded Mistake

Jace had always been told that guns weren't toys, but when his cousin Malik pulled one out from under his bed, it didn't seem real. The metal felt heavier than he expected, the grip cold against his palm.

"Go ahead, check it out," Malik grinned, spinning the gun on the floor like it was some kind of prize.

Jace hesitated. "It's not loaded, right?"

Malik shrugged. "I don't think so."

That answer wasn't good enough. Jace had seen too many news stories about kids who thought the same thing, only to make a mistake they could never undo. But he didn't want to look scared. His fingers traced the trigger, just to feel what it was like.

And then—click.

The sound echoed in the small room. Jace's heart slammed against his ribs. He nearly dropped the gun.

Malik's face drained of color. "Dude—"

Jace didn't wait to hear the rest. He shoved the gun back into the drawer and backed away. His hands were shaking. If there had been a bullet inside… if he had pulled any harder…

His knees felt weak. "I'm out, man. I'm not messing with that thing."

That night, Jace couldn't sleep. He kept picturing what could've happened—what almost did. And he knew one thing for sure: that was the last time he'd ever touch a gun.

Moral:

One bad decision can change—or end—a life. Guns aren't toys.

The First Cigarette

"Come on, it's just one puff."

Lexi stood in the cold night air, her best friend Sierra holding out the cigarette like an invitation to some exclusive club. The guys standing around them had already lit up, exhaling clouds of smoke that swirled under the streetlights.

Lexi hesitated. Her mom used to smoke—until the doctor found the spot on her lung. She remembered the nights of coughing that shook the walls, the way her mom's voice turned raspy, the oxygen tank in the corner of their living room.

But that was different, right? This was just one.

She took the cigarette between her fingers. Sierra grinned. "That's my girl."

Lexi brought it to her lips, the acrid scent burning her nose. She inhaled—and immediately doubled over, hacking. Her throat burned. Her chest felt tight, like she was breathing in fire instead of air.

The guys laughed. "Damn, first time?"

Sierra smacked her back. "You get used to it."

Lexi straightened, her eyes watering. No, she wouldn't. She saw her mom's face in her head, the exhausted eyes, the regret. She shoved the cigarette back at Sierra.

"I'm good," she rasped.

Sierra frowned. "Really? It's just one."

Lexi coughed again. "Yeah, and that's one too many."

She walked away, her throat raw but her mind clear. That wasn't a path she wanted to go down. She'd already seen where it led.

Moral:

Every habit starts with 'just one'—until it's not just one anymore.

The Dropout Decision

Damien stared at the test in front of him—another F. He wasn't surprised. He hadn't done the homework, hadn't studied, hadn't even paid attention in class.

What was the point? School wasn't for him. He was just tired of the whole routine—wake up, go to school, do the work, fail, repeat. It felt pointless. Every time he tried, it seemed like nothing changed.

At lunch, he told his best friend, Trey, "I'm done. I'm dropping out."

Trey nearly choked on his soda. "Dude, what?"

"I mean it." Damien leaned back in his chair, tapping his fingers on the table. "School's a waste of time. I'll just get a job. Who needs a diploma anyway?"

Trey blinked, clearly surprised. "Wait, are you seriously saying you're dropping out? What about your future, bro?"

Damien shrugged. "I'll figure it out. Maybe I'll get a job at a place that doesn't care about my grades. Something easy. Stock shelves, work in fast food, whatever. It's not like I'm gonna be some bigshot anyway."

Trey was quiet for a moment, clearly thinking hard. "But... where's that gonna get you in a few years, man?"

Damien rolled his eyes. "I don't know, Trey. I'm done with school. It's just not for me."

A week later, Damien found himself stocking shelves at a grocery store. It wasn't glamorous, but it paid enough to keep his gas tank full and cover his basic needs. He worked long hours, but it felt like freedom. No more school. No more deadlines. Just the steady rhythm of work.

But by the time Damien turned 19, he realized his friends had moved on. Most of them had gone to college, enrolled in trade schools, or gotten into programs that could set them up for better jobs. They were getting certifications and making plans. Trey was one of them.

One night, after a ten-hour shift, Damien walked into the gas station to grab a drink. He spotted Trey filling up his car, wearing a set of scrubs. Damien raised an eyebrow.

"Yo, you working at the hospital?"

Trey grinned, adjusting the straps of his scrubs. "Yeah, man. I'm doing the CNA program right now." He paused, glancing at his friend. "I get to work with patients, and I'm making decent money already. In about a year, I'll be a nurse."

Damien's heart sank. He looked down at his worn-out grocery store uniform. He'd been stuck in the same job for over a year, while Trey was on track to make something of himself. That could've been him, if he hadn't dropped out so quickly. He could've been working his way up, too.

"Damn," Damien muttered under his breath.

Trey noticed the look on his face and took a step closer. "You okay, man?"

Damien took a deep breath, then shook his head. "I could've been doing something like that, right? If I just finished school..."

Trey gave a sympathetic smile. "It's never too late, dude. You can still go back and finish your GED."

Damien blinked. "GED? What's that?"

Trey grinned. "You didn't know? The GED stands for General Educational Development. It's a test you can take if you didn't finish high school. If you pass it, it's like you got your high school diploma. You can use it to apply for better jobs or get into college or trade school."

Damien felt a spark of hope flicker inside him. "So, I can still get a diploma without going back to school?"

"Exactly. And trust me, man, you don't want to be stuck in dead-end jobs forever. You've got the potential. You just have to take that first step."

That night, Damien sat down at his computer and typed four words into Google: How to get a GED. The search results came up with links to study guides, test centers, and stories of people who had taken the test after dropping out. It didn't seem too hard. He could study on his own time, and there were plenty of places to take the test.

By the time he went to bed, Damien had already made up his mind. He wasn't going to let his past decisions hold him back any longer. He was going to take the test, get his GED, and start planning for a better future.

The next morning, he woke up with a new sense of purpose. He called Trey to thank him for the encouragement and to let him know about his decision. Trey was hyped for him. "I knew you'd come around, man! You've got this!"

Damien smiled for the first time in a while. He felt the weight of regret lifting off his shoulders.

Moral:

Dropping out might feel like freedom now, but later, it feels like regret. There are always second chances if you're willing to take them. The GED can be the first step toward a better future.

The Joyride That Wasn't

Devin's phone buzzed. "Yo, got my brother's car. Let's go."

His heart pounded with excitement as he grabbed his hoodie and slipped out the door. He wasn't even thinking about the fact that Jordan, his best friend, didn't have a license. Jordan's brother worked nights, and the keys were always sitting on the counter. "Borrowing" the car was practically tradition by now.

By the time Devin reached the parking lot, the engine was already rumbling. Jordan smirked from the driver's seat. "You ready?"

Devin hesitated. "You sure about this?"

Jordan scoffed. "Relax, man. I've driven plenty of times."

That wasn't exactly true. Devin had seen Jordan mess around in empty parking lots, maybe take a few back roads, but driving at night, on real streets? That was different. Still, Devin ignored the uneasy feeling gnawing at his gut and climbed into the passenger seat.

At first, it was fun. The wind whipped through the open windows, music blasted from the speakers, and for a few minutes, it felt like they owned the night.

Then Jordan pushed the gas pedal harder.

"Chill, bro," Devin muttered, gripping the seat.

Jordan laughed. "You scared?"

The streetlights blurred as they sped past. A red light appeared ahead, but Jordan barely slowed down.

And then—screech.

A car turned in front of them. Jordan yanked the wheel hard, and the world spun. Tires screamed. Metal crunched.

Then—silence.

Devin's chest heaved. He was still in the car, but the hood was crumpled, smoke hissing from the engine. Jordan was gripping the wheel, his face pale.

A man from the other car was shouting. Sirens wailed in the distance.

Jordan's voice was barely a whisper. "We're screwed."

Devin swallowed hard, his hands shaking. His mom's face flashed in his mind. His future. His freedom. All of it—gone—because of one stupid decision.

As the red and blue lights painted the night, Devin realized something: This wasn't a joyride. It was a nightmare.

Moral:

One reckless choice can cost you your freedom, your future, or even your life.

The Price of Brotherhood

Jalen wiped the sweat from his palms onto his jeans as he stood on the corner. The streetlights buzzed overhead, casting long shadows on the cracked pavement. His heart pounded so loud he was sure Malik and the others could hear it.

"You sure about this?" Malik asked, flipping a lighter open and shut. The flame flared for a second before vanishing.

Jalen nodded, even though his stomach was twisting into knots. "Yeah," he lied.

For weeks, he had been standing on the sidelines, watching the guys in Shadow Kings—his older cousin's crew—walk through school like they owned the place. No one messed with them. No one laughed at them. And unlike Jalen, they never had to count their dollars before buying lunch.

"I gotta do this," Jalen had told himself over and over again. His mom was working two jobs just to keep their apartment. His little sister needed school supplies. And he was tired of feeling powerless.

"Alright," Malik said, nodding toward a beat-up sedan parked down the street. "See that car? Belongs to some dude from another block. He owes us. Go slash his tires."

Jalen swallowed. "What?"

Malik smirked. "You wanna be one of us, you gotta prove you got the heart for it."

Jalen's hands clenched into fists. He had expected something big, but this? His mind raced. What if the guy caught him? What if someone called the cops? But then he thought about Malik's words: You wanna be one of us?

That's what he wanted, right? To be respected. To be untouchable.

Before he could talk himself out of it, Jalen took the knife Malik handed him and walked toward the car. Every step felt heavier than the last. His fingers shook as he crouched down near the front tire.

Then—footsteps.

Jalen spun around just as a deep voice cut through the night. "What the hell you doin'?"

A man stood in the doorway of a nearby building, arms crossed, eyes locked onto him. He wasn't some stranger. Jalen recognized him—Dre, one of the older guys from the neighborhood. The same guy who used to shoot hoops with Jalen and his friends at the park.

Jalen's breath came in short, sharp bursts. His fingers gripped the knife, but his whole body screamed at him to run.

Dre stepped closer. "That's your big move? Cutting some dude's tires so a bunch of fools will let you in their little crew?" He scoffed. "You think they got your back?"

Jalen's mind flashed to Malik and the others, standing in the distance, waiting to see if he'd do it. Would they help him if things went wrong? If he got locked up?

Dre's voice was softer now. "They're not your brothers, man. Trust me."

Jalen looked back at the car, at his reflection in the cracked side mirror. His hands were still shaking. His heart was still racing. But now, it wasn't from excitement—it was from fear. Not of getting caught. Not of Malik.

But of becoming someone he wouldn't recognize.

Slowly, he dropped the knife.

He didn't look back as he walked away. He didn't have to. He already knew—Malik and his crew would be laughing, calling him weak. But for the first time in a long time, Jalen didn't feel weak. He felt free.

Moral:

Real strength isn't proving yourself to others—it's knowing when to walk away.

The High Cost

Jalen was known for his smooth confidence. On the basketball court, he was electric. Coaches talked about college scouts. Teachers praised his leadership. But lately, that version of Jalen had been slipping.

It started with a smoke circle behind the gym—"just a hit" with some friends after practice. He didn't see the harm. "It's just weed," his boy Malik said. "It's legal in some places. No big deal."

Jalen liked the way it slowed his mind. No pressure. No stress. So he hit it again. And again.

Over time, the gym became optional. He showed up to school smelling like smoke, eyes glazed. His coach benched him for a game—then two. His mom noticed too, confronting him after a call from the school.

"You're throwing it away, Jalen," she said.

"I'm just relaxing," he mumbled. "Everyone does it."

Then came the showcase game—the one with scouts in the stands. He promised himself he wouldn't smoke that week. But the anxiety got to him. He needed to chill out the night before. Just one more time.

During the game, Jalen was slow. Disconnected. He missed easy passes. Airballed a free throw. He sat on the bench, watching another player take his place—someone hungry, focused.

The scouts never came back.

Later, alone in the locker room, Jalen looked at his jersey. His future. Everything he'd let slip.

Moral:

What feels like an escape can become a trap. Short-term relief isn't worth long-term regret. Stay sharp. Stay focused. Your dreams need you clear-headed.

Filtered Reality

An original short story by Tequila Smith

Theme: Social Media Pressure, Self-Worth, and Comparison

Story:

Seventeen-year-old Amaya scrolled through her feed under the covers, the blue glow from her phone lighting up the dark room. It was past midnight—again. But she couldn't look away.

Every swipe showed her someone doing more.

"Accepted to NYU! Full ride!"

"My boyfriend just surprised me with a promise ring."

"Skin glowing, stress-free, and living my best life."

Amaya double-tapped, even though the posts made her chest tighten. Her life didn't look like that. At all.

Her grades were slipping, her parents were arguing more lately, and her hair hadn't cooperated in weeks. She posted a selfie last week that only got 34 likes. She deleted it after an hour. Too embarrassing.

At school, she smiled, nodded, and laughed at the right times. But inside, she felt invisible. Or worse—unseen.

Her best friend, Zora, barely posted and didn't care. "That stuff's fake, Maya," she said once. "Filters, editing, timing—none of it's real."

"But it feels real," Amaya whispered.

One day in class, they were assigned a digital detox challenge: no social media for 48 hours. Most students groaned. Amaya panicked.

"Just try," Zora said. "Your brain needs a break."

That night, Amaya stared at her phone. Her fingers hovered over the app. She turned it off. She couldn't sleep.

Day one felt like withdrawal. She reached for her phone every ten minutes out of habit. She kept wondering:

What am I missing?

Are people noticing I'm not posting?

What if they forget me?

But by day two, something shifted.

She finished a book she'd been meaning to read. She sketched in her notebook. She helped her little brother build a Lego castle. She laughed—really laughed—with Zora at lunch instead of staring at a screen.

That night, she looked in the mirror. Her face, bare and unfiltered, smiled back. It wasn't perfect, but it was hers.

When the 48 hours ended, she opened the app again—but something felt different. The pictures didn't feel like truth anymore. They felt like props. Like pressure.

She posted a picture of her sketch, no filter, no makeup, no front.

The caption read:

"No filter. No mask. Just me."

It didn't go viral. But for once, she didn't care.

Moral:

Social media shows us the highlight reel, not the behind-the-scenes. Don't let filtered perfection define your worth. Real life isn't always picture perfect—and that's what makes it beautiful.

The Weight No One Saw

Jordan was the funny kid. The one who always had a comeback, always got the teacher to crack a smile. He wore confidence like a hoodie—oversized and a little worn, but comfortable.

What no one saw was the way he stayed up at night, eyes wide, fighting thoughts that came like waves. Some days, just brushing his teeth felt like climbing a mountain.

He didn't know how to say, "I'm not okay." Because how could someone who always made others laugh be the one struggling?

He tried to fake his way through it. He smiled harder. Laughed louder. But the silence when he got home screamed louder than anything.

Until one day, in the middle of English class, he just... broke. A tear slipped. He tried to hide it, but Mr. Reaves saw.

After class, Mr. Reaves pulled him aside. "You don't have to carry it alone," he said gently. "You matter. You deserve to feel better."

It was the first time someone looked past the jokes and saw him.

That day, Jordan asked for help. Counseling. Support. Space to heal. It didn't fix everything overnight—but it was the first day he didn't feel alone.

Moral:

Depression doesn't always look like sadness. Sometimes it looks like silence behind a smile. It's okay to not be okay—and it's brave to ask for help.

Behind Closed Doors

Talia was a sophomore—smart, low-key, with a style that was more hoodies and hoops than lip gloss and lashes. Ron was a family friend. Someone everyone trusted, who smiled in public but whispered wrong things when no one was around.

At first, she thought maybe she was imagining it. Then she told herself it was her fault—maybe she didn't say "stop" loud enough.

To most people, Ron was cool. He coached her little brother's soccer team, fixed stuff around the house, and always brought Talia snacks when she was studying. At first, she didn't mind him being around. He was chill. Funny. Safe.

But lately, things started to feel... off.

It started small—compliments that lingered. "You're really growing up. Starting to look like a woman," he said once, eyes resting too long. Then there were the late-night "accidental" brushes when they passed in the hallway. The way he started asking for hugs more often. How he'd comment on her outfits seemed weird.

She told herself she was overthinking it. He hadn't done anything— at least, that's what she tried to believe.

One night, while her mom worked the overnight shift, Ron knocked on her door.

"Just wanted to check on you," he said. But when he sat on her bed and didn't leave, her stomach dropped.

Talia locked herself in the bathroom afterward, her hands shaking. She didn't know what to call it. She felt gross. Confused. Guilty for even thinking something was wrong.

That night, she DM'd her cousin Nia and told her everything.

Nia didn't say "Are you sure?"

She said: "That's not okay. I believe you. Tell someone."

The next day, Talia asked to speak to the school counselor, Ms. Brooks. Her voice trembled, but she got the words out.

"He keeps coming into my room. He touches me sometimes. Not like… crazy, but just enough to make me feel like I'm not safe."

Ms. Brooks didn't question her feelings. She just nodded, and said, "You did the right thing by telling me. You are not to blame. I'm going to help you."

From there, things moved quickly. CPS was called. Talia's mom was shocked—but she believed her. Ron was removed from the home. And slowly, life began to feel safe again.

Talia started therapy. There were bad days, nightmares, and moments she felt broken. But there were also days she wrote poems, painted out her pain, and even led a presentation for her school's awareness week on boundaries and consent.

She learned that grooming wasn't always about force—it was about control. About making someone doubt their instincts. But she also learned that instincts are powerful. And when she listened to hers, she found freedom.

Moral:

If someone's making you feel unsafe—even if they're "family" or someone everyone trusts—you are allowed to speak up. Telling the truth is not betrayal—it's bravery. You are never to blame for someone else's wrong behavior. Your voice is powerful, and some people will believe you, help you and protect you.

Not Just a Hashtag

Cameron was popular online. His TikToks had thousands of likes. Everyone said he was "that guy"—cool, confident, funny.

But one night, after posting a video with a forced smile, Cameron stared at his phone... and then his ceiling... and then a bottle of pills.

The emptiness wouldn't go away.

He typed a note in his phone:

"I don't think I belong here anymore."

He hit post.

But his little sister, Ava, walked in just in time. She saw his face— pale, quiet, still. She screamed.

They rushed him to the hospital. He survived.

In recovery, Cameron admitted something he never had before: he didn't want to die—he just wanted the pain to stop.

The next time he posted, it was raw and real. No music. No filter.

"I'm not okay. But I'm here. And I'm learning to live one breath at a time."

Comments flooded in:

"Me too."

"Thank you."

"You helped me speak up."

That post saved others. And it helped Cameron start saving himself.

Moral:

Suicide is a silence that doesn't have to win. Even when your mind says you don't matter—**you do**. One honest conversation can change everything. This world is better because you're in it.

Name Without a Label

Fourteen-year-old Elijah sat on the edge of his bed, staring at the ceiling, a storm of thoughts swirling in his head. Some days, he felt like he fit in with the boys in class. Other days, he felt completely different—like he was walking in someone else's shoes.

He wasn't sure if he liked girls. Or boys. Or both. Or maybe… he just didn't know how to explain it.

He tried googling words like "bi," "nonbinary," "fluid." Some of it felt right. Most of it felt confusing.

At school, he smiled and played the part. But at night, he felt like he was floating in a question mark.

For a while, Elijah told no one. Not even his best friend. What if they didn't understand? What if he was just imagining it?

But the weight got heavier. His chest tightened more often. He couldn't concentrate in class. He started avoiding the mirror.

Then one day, during free period, he walked into the counselor's office.

"I don't really know why I'm here," he mumbled.

Mrs. Ramirez smiled gently. "That's okay. You showed up. That's a start."

They sat in silence for a few moments before Elijah blurted, "I think I'm confused about who I like… or who I am."

Mrs. Ramirez didn't flinch. "A lot of teens feel that way. You don't need to have it all figured out to talk about it."

That one sentence let Elijah breathe. For the first time in weeks, he didn't feel broken—just curious.

Over the next few weeks, they talked more. Slowly, Elijah started talking to his mom too. He'd been scared she'd be disappointed. But when he finally told her, she pulled him into a hug and whispered, "I love you. Always. No matter what name or label you choose—if you even choose one."

The fog didn't disappear overnight. But Elijah wasn't walking through it alone anymore. He was talking, processing, growing.

And maybe that was the whole point—not finding all the answers, but learning how to ask the questions without shame.

Moral:

You don't have to figure out who you are all by yourself. Talking to someone safe—like a parent, counselor, or trusted adult—can help you find clarity, confidence, and peace in your journey.

The Mirror and the Scroll

Amira used to love mirrors. When she was younger, she'd twirl in front of them, cheeks puffed with laughter, imagining she was on the cover of a magazine.

But now, at fifteen, the mirror made her feel more like a glitch in a filtered world.

Her forehead had broken out again. Her thighs touched when she walked. Her curls, thick and rebellious, didn't fall like the slick ponytails she scrolled past on TikTok. Everyone online seemed to have the look—clear skin, tiny waists, perfectly edited smiles. And even though she knew it was fake sometimes, it still got in her head.

"You're so pretty," her friends would say, but all Amira saw were flaws.

One day, she found herself scrolling for hours—before and afters, glow-ups, weight loss videos, makeup hacks. She looked up and realized it was dark outside. She'd wasted the whole day comparing herself.

That night, she got brave and opened up to her older brother Malik.

"I don't get it. I try so hard, but I still don't look like them. It's like… I'll never be enough," she said, voice cracking.

Malik, who was an art major, walked into his room and came back with a painting he'd made. It was bold and abstract—curves, color, texture, all woven into a chaotic, beautiful piece.

"What do you think?" he asked.

"It's beautiful," she said.

"Even though it's not perfect?"

She nodded slowly.

"That's how I see you, Mira. Not made to be a copy. Not made to be flat or polished. But full of dimension. Real. Raw. Beautiful because you're you."

His words didn't erase her insecurities overnight—but they cracked the mirror. Just a little.

Amira started doing one small thing each day: saying something kind to herself out loud. She unfollowed accounts that made her feel like less. She began creating content that showed her in real life—laughing with braces, dancing in oversized hoodies, sharing her poetry.

People responded.

"So relatable."

"I needed this."

"You're beautiful."

But the most important comment came from herself:

"I'm starting to believe it."

Moral:

The world will always try to tell you who to be—but the most powerful glow-up comes when you love who you already are. You don't need to look like anyone else to be worthy, seen, or enough. Real is beautiful. So are you.

The Wrong Turn

Seventeen-year-old Tasha was sick of being yelled at.

Every day it was something:
"Your grades are slipping again."
"You got another referral?"
"How many times do we have to tell you — stay off your phone during school!"
"Why didn't you take out the trash like I asked?"
"Those girls you hang out with? Trouble."

And when she got suspended for skipping class and mouthing off to a teacher, her parents lost it. They took her phone, shut down her social media accounts, and told her she was grounded for a month. No parties. No hanging out. No freedom.

Tasha felt like a prisoner in her own house.

"I'm not even doing anything that bad!" she screamed one night. "Y'all treat me like I'm some criminal!"

"We're trying to save you from making choices you'll regret," her mom said.

But Tasha didn't want to hear it. She was tired of being controlled.

That night, with nothing but a backpack and her anger, she climbed out of her bedroom window and left. She didn't have a plan — just a will to get away.

A girl she followed on Instagram, Kaylee, had posted about a place in another city where "teens can make real money, no parents, no rules." Tasha DM'd her.

Kaylee was all smiles and promises. "You'll be living your best life, girl. I'll come get you."

And she did.

At first, it felt like freedom — cheap hotels, no curfew, and new clothes. But soon, the truth hit: the job was a trap. Kaylee wasn't just a friend — she was part of a trafficking ring, and Tasha was the next victim.

Her phone was gone again, but this time not by choice. She wasn't allowed to leave. She was being watched. The things they made her do were things she never imagined — things she couldn't talk about.

Tasha remembered the fights at home — and how small they felt compared to this.

But she also remembered something her mom once said: "Even if you mess up, we will always love you. Just come back."

When one of the men fell asleep with his phone still in his hand, Tasha took a chance. She sent a short message to 911 with the address. She didn't know if it would work — but it did.

Within hours, police rescued her. Kaylee was arrested, along with the men who had been exploiting girls like her.

Tasha was placed in a recovery home where counselors helped her process the trauma. She wasn't the same. She was stronger — and more aware.

Weeks later, her parents came to see her. They cried. They hugged her. They weren't angry — they were grateful she was alive.

Now, Tasha shares her story with others:

"I thought my parents were the enemy. I thought discipline was control. But I didn't see the danger waiting outside my door. If you're thinking about running — don't. That wrong turn could cost you everything."

Moral:

Being corrected isn't being controlled — it's being cared for. Poor choices can lead to real danger, but there's power in using your voice. Stand up. Speak out. No regrets.

Reflective questions:

What was the turning point in the story?

How did the main character grow or change?

Was there a moment when things could have gone differently?

What lesson did this story teach you?

How can you apply this lesson in your own life?

Understanding the Story

What tough decision did the main character face?

What kind of pressure did they feel, and who was influencing them?

What were the possible consequences of both the right and wrong choices?

In your opinion, what was the turning point in the story?

Personal Reflection

Have you ever been in a situation like this? What did you do?

How do you think you would have reacted if you were in the character's shoes?

What do you think the character learned from this experience?

Do you think it's easy or hard to stand up for what's right when everyone else is silent? Why?

Social Impact

How do peer decisions affect the school or community around them?

What role does silence play in making a bad situation worse?

How can one person's decision influence others in a positive way?

Values and Morals

Why do you think doing the right thing is sometimes the hardest choice?

What values do you think are most important when facing peer pressure?

How can someone build the courage to say "no" when it's unpopular?

Long-Term Thinking

What do you think this story teaches about character and reputation?

Can one bad decision affect your future? How?

Why is it important to think about long-term consequences and not just the moment?

Support System

Who do you trust to talk to if you're ever in a tough situation?

How can friends support each other in making better choices?

What would you say to someone who's pressuring others to make bad decisions?

Important Resources for Support

No matter what you're going through, it's essential to remember that you're never alone. Whether you're struggling with your emotions, facing difficulties in your relationships, or dealing with challenges that feel too big to handle, help is always available.

Reaching out to someone you trust—whether it's a parent, a friend, or a professional—can make all the difference. Sometimes, taking that first step to talk can feel difficult, but it's a powerful moment of strength. The following resources are here for you, 24/7, whenever you need them. Don't hesitate to reach out. Remember, this world is better because you are in it.

You matter. Your voice matters. Your well-being matters.

Emergency and Crisis Hotlines

1. **National Suicide Prevention Lifeline Phone:** 988 (Text or Call) **Website:** 988lifeline.org Provides 24/7 free and confidential support for people in distress, prevention, and crisis resources.

2. **Crisis Text Line Text:** 741741 **Website:** crisistextline.org 24/7 text-based support for people in crisis.

3. **National Domestic Violence Hotline Phone:** 1-800-799-SAFE (1-800-799-7233) **Website:** thehotline.org Provides confidential support for survivors of domestic violence, including texting options.

4. **National Child Abuse Hotline Phone:** 1-800-4-A-CHILD (1-800-422-4453) **Website:** childhelp.org Offers 24/7 confidential help for children, parents, and adults dealing with child abuse or neglect.

5. **RAINN (Rape, Abuse & Incest National Network) Phone:** 1-800-656-HOPE (1-800-656-4673) **Website:** rainn.org A 24/7 hotline that provides confidential support for sexual assault survivors and those affected.

Mental Health and Counseling Support

6. **Teen Line Phone:** 310-855-HOPE (310-855-4673) **Text:** TEEN to 839863 **Website:** teenlineonline.org A peer-to-peer hotline for teens, offering confidential support for mental health, relationships, and more.

7. **National Alliance on Mental Illness (NAMI) Phone:** 1-800-950-NAMI (1-800-950-6264) **Website:** nami.org Provides information and support for mental health issues, including depression and anxiety.

8. **SAMHSA National Helpline (Substance Abuse and Mental Health Services) Phone:** 1-800-662-HELP (1-800-662-4357) **Website:** samhsa.gov A free, confidential helpline for individuals and families facing mental health or substance use disorders.

Bullying and LGBTQ+ Support

9. **StopBullying.gov Website:** stopbullying.gov Resources and information on how to stop bullying, report bullying, and support kids and teens facing bullying.

10. **The Trevor Project (LGBTQ+ Youth Crisis Support) Phone:** 1-866-488-7386 **Text:** Text START to 678678 **Website:** thetrevorproject.org Offers confidential support for LGBTQ+ youth in crisis, including suicide prevention and resources.

Drug and Alcohol Abuse Help

11. **National Institute on Drug Abuse (NIDA) Helpline Phone:** 1-800-662-HELP (1-800-662-4357) **Website:** drugabuse.gov Provides support for those struggling with substance abuse, including referrals to treatment services.

12. **SMART Recovery (Self-Management and Recovery Training) Website:** smartrecovery.org Provides free and confidential online support for individuals struggling with addiction, including online meetings.

General Teen Support

13. **Boys Town National Hotline Phone:** 1-800-448-3000 **Website:** boystown.org Provides crisis support for teens, helping them with bullying, family struggles, and mental health issues.

14. **National Runaway Safeline Phone:** 1-800-RUNAWAY (1-800-786-2929) **Website:** 1800runaway.org A 24/7 helpline for youth in crisis, offering help with runaway situations and emotional distress.

Online Resources for Support and Awareness

15. **My Strength (Mental Health and Wellness App) Website:** mystrength.com Offers tools and resources for mental health, mindfulness, and substance abuse recovery.

16. **Love is respect (Relationship Violence Support) Phone:** 1-866-331-9474 **Text:** Text "LOVEIS" to 22522 **Website:** loveisrespect.org Provides resources for teens experiencing unhealthy relationships, dating violence, and abuse.